What Do You Think a Cat Would See

Author: Heather Noelle

Illustrator: K. Nicole

AuthorHouse™
1663 Liberty Drive
Bloomington, IN 47403
www.authorhouse.com
Phone: 1 (800) 839-8640

Because of the dynamic nature of the Internet, any web addresses or links contained in this book may have changed
since publication and may no longer be valid. The views expressed in this work are solely those of the author and do
not necessarily reflect the views of the publisher, and the publisher hereby disclaims any responsibility for them.

Any people depicted in stock imagery provided by Getty Images are models,
and such images are being used for illustrative purposes only.
Certain stock imagery © Getty Images.

This book is printed on acid-free paper.

ISBN: 978-1-7283-6424-7 (sc)
ISBN: 978-1-7283-6423-0 (e)

Library of Congress Control Number: 2020910771

Print information available on the last page.

Published by AuthorHouse 06/19/2020

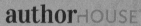

This book is dedicated to my large EATM cats, Kissu, Jodie, Chad and the little furry kitty whom I caught wandering the streets, the night I received inspiration for this book.

After the sun has gone to bed,
with colors full of orange and red,
we lock our doors and go to sleep,
while the cats outside wait in the street.

What do you think a cat would see?
It's dark outside too dark for me.
Amongst the bushes without a fright,
a cat can wander throughout the night.

What do you think a cat would see?
Where do you think a cat would be?

There's Mr. Wilson down the lane,
the cat looks in through the window pane.
He moves on by no time to stop,
there're trees to climb and leaves to bop.

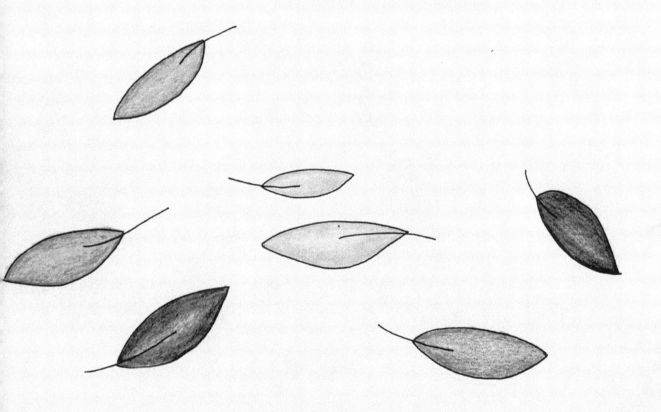

What do you think a cat would see?
Where do you think a cat would be?

Sweet Mrs. Rose has left a treat,
some tasty milk that can't be beat.

The cat moves on to meet some friends,
just down the street where the willow bends.

The moon lights up the night sky
he wanders on, that crazy guy!
He sees a squirrel, or wait a mouse?
It ran behind that little house.

What do you think a cat would see?
Where do you think a cat would be?
He walks in the garden
and rolls in the sand...

...He runs atop the garbage cans.

As the moon dips down and the sun comes up,
his nighttime play is about to stop.

What do you think a cat would see?
Where do you think a cat would be?

He sits and listens to the wind,
that tells him stories of where it's been.

He won't get lost, he can't you see,
my cat knows exactly where he is supposed to be.

CPSIA information can be obtained
at www.ICGtesting.com
Printed in the USA
BVHW020945020720
582816BV00017B/1938